NICK JR.

The BACKYARDIGANS™

Secret Agents

adapted by Wendy Wax
based on the original teleplay "Secret Mission"
by McPaul Smith
illustrated by Zina Saunders

SIMON AND SCHUSTER/NICKELODEON

Based on the TV series *Nick Jr. The Backyardigans*™ as seen on Nick Jr

SIMON AND SCHUSTER
First published in Great Britain in 2008 by Simon & Schuster UK Ltd
Africa House, 64-78 Kingsway, London WC2B 6AH

Originally published in the USA in 2006 by Simon Spotlight,
an imprint of Simon & Schuster Children's Division, New York.

A CIP catalogue record for this book is available from the British Library

ISBN 978-1-84738-222-1

Printed in China

10 9 8 7 6 5 4 3 2 1

Visit our websites: www.simonsays.co.uk
                    www.nickjr.co.uk

Pablo peeked out from behind a tree.

"Shh, I'm Agent Pablo – a *secret* agent. Secret agents go on secret missions!"

Tyrone crept out from behind a bush. "I'm Agent Tyrone!" he said.
"All clear, Agent Pablo?"
   "All clear, Agent Tyrone!" said Pablo.

Just then Uniqua sneaked out from behind a bush.
"I'm Agent Uniqua," she said, "and I'm extremely sneaky!"

"What is our secret mission, Agent Pablo?" asked Tyrone.
Pablo held up a box with a bone inside it. "We need to sneak into the Treasure Museum to return this mystery bone to its secret owner," he said.

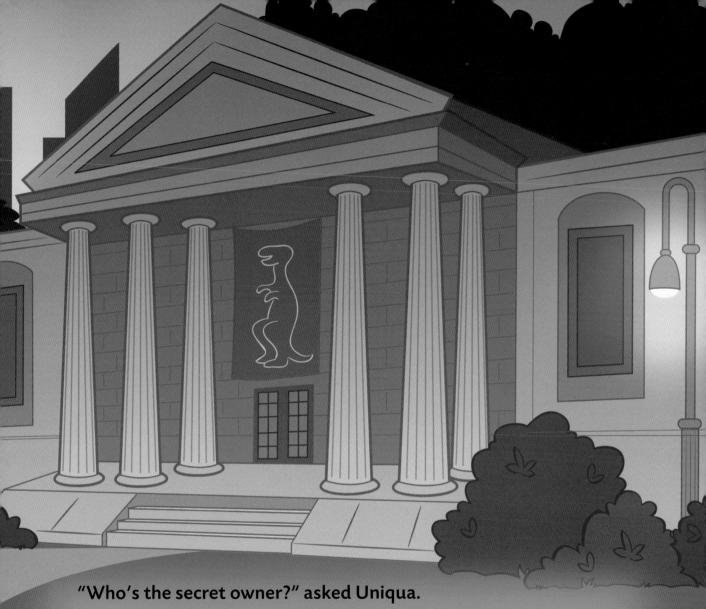

"Who's the secret owner?" asked Uniqua.

"I don't know," Pablo said. "It's a secret, but he's in the
Treasure Museum."

"But the Treasure Museum has alarms and booby traps!" said Tyrone.

"Secret agents can *always* find a way to sneak in," said Uniqua.

Outside the Treasure Museum, Pablo showed the other agents his spy gadget. It was small with lots of top-secret buttons. Uniqua had brought a spy power rope to help them in tough situations. Tyrone had brought a bottle of maple syrup.

"Maple syrup!" said Pablo and Uniqua. "What's that for?"
"It's spy maple syrup," said Tyrone. "In case we need something sticky."

"Let's go," said Uniqua.

"Secret agents never just *go* in. They *sneak* in!" said Pablo. He used his spy gadget to open a secret trap door at their feet.

"How will we get down there?" asked Tyrone.
"No problem! With my spy power rope!" said Uniqua. "Grab on, agents! We're going down!"

The secret agents found themselves in the Hall of Precious Jewels.

"Rubies, emeralds, and pearls!" said Tyrone. "These certainly are precious jewels."

"Watch out for alarms and booby traps in here," said Pablo. "Look! This must be the biggest diamond in the world," Uniqua exclaimed, turning to her friends. But in her excitement, she bumped into the stand that held the huge diamond. "Watch out!" Pablo cried, as the diamond fell.

Tyrone caught the diamond – just as a cage fell down from the ceiling. *Clank!*

"Oh, no!" cried Uniqua. "A booby trap!"

"We're trapped!" cried Pablo, starting to panic. "Uh-oh! Secret agents should never get trapped. But we're trapped. Uh-oh . . ."

"Pablo!" said Uniqua. "Calm down. We have to be cool and think."

"We *could* try my spy maple syrup," suggested Tyrone.

"Nah," said Uniqua and Pablo.

"Maybe if we put the diamond back, the cage will go up," said Uniqua.
Pablo pressed a button on his spy gadget. A mechanical arm with
a claw grabbed the diamond and returned it to its base – and the cage
began to rise.

The agents came to a doorway. Three laser beams blocked their way.

"If we touch the laser beams, we'll set off an alarm!" warned Pablo.

"But how do we get past them?" asked Tyrone.

"We've got to do the limbo under the beams," said Pablo.

After they carefully went under the laser beams, the secret agents came upon the Gargantuan Gallery.

"How will we find the secret owner of the mystery bone?" Uniqua asked.

Just then she tripped over a dinosaur's foot. It was missing a baby toe.

"You found him!" said Pablo. "The mystery bone is the dinosaur's toe!"

"We need something sticky to attach the toe to the foot," said Uniqua.

"I *knew* my spy maple syrup would come in handy," said Tyrone. He stuck the bone in place. "Mission accomplished!"

"Let's get out of here!" said Tyrone.
Uniqua shot the spy power rope up through the skylight.
"Grab hold, agents!" she said. "Going up!"

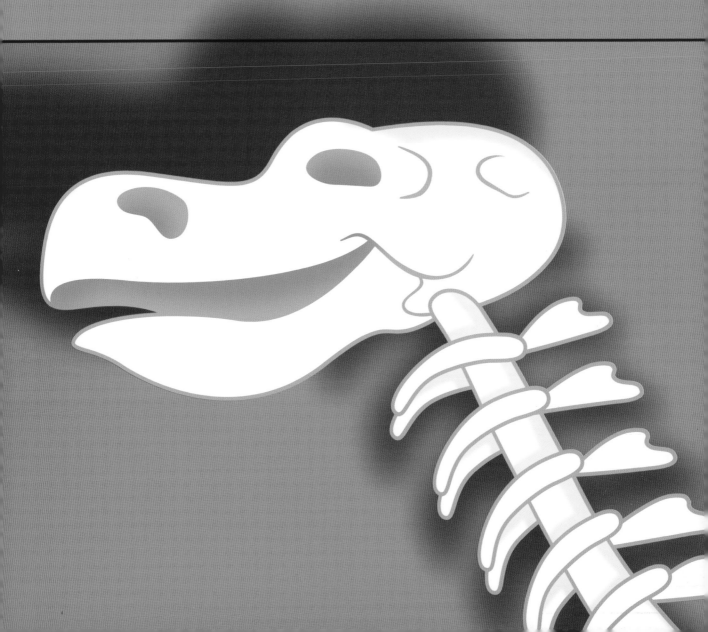

"That was quite a mysterious adventure!" said Tyrone.

"And very sneaky," said Uniqua.

"Now let's have a snack at my house!"

So off they all went for a secret agent snack.